I'm a JETS' fan

_____

Fuelled by Passion!

The HOME Team

Written by Holly Preston
Illustrated by Val Lawton

Always  Books

The Home Team

Text © 2012 Holly Preston
Illustrations © 2012 Val Lawton

Manufactured by Friesens Corporation in Altona, MB, Canada
September 2012
Job #75455

Library and Archives Canada Cataloguing in Publication

Preston, Holly
The home team / written by Holly Preston ; illustrated by Val Lawton.

ISBN 978-0-9869244-1-5

I. Lawton, Val, 1962- II. Title.

PS8631.R467H64 2012   jC813'.6   C2012-904947-6

Layout by Heather Nickel

With many thanks to the Winnipeg Jets.

Jets Gear, the Authentic Team Store of the Winnipeg Jets Hockey Club is proud to bring to you this Exclusive Item, available only at Jets Gear. Thorough development by team officials ensures that this item meets the precise specifications of the Winnipeg Jets. Profits from the sale of goods purchased at Jets Gear are invested directly back into the Winnipeg Jets Hockey Club, supporting the pursuit of their ultimate goal of bringing the Stanley Cup to Winnipeg.

Support your Home Team, Shop Where the Players Shop.

MIX
Paper from responsible sources
FSC® C016245

Always Books

For all young JETS' fans who know there's no place like home!

There was nothing better than playing hockey.

Liam, Sophia, Ethan and Logan called themselves the Junior **JETS**.

On days when there was no school, they'd start in the morning …

… and they'd play till night.

And even then, Liam thought only about … hockey.
He may have been the smallest on the team,
but his hockey dreams were big.

The only problem was Liam never scored. Ever.
The puck went high. The puck went low.
The puck went everywhere but where it was supposed to go.

"The **JETS** were little boys once, too, Liam," his dad said. "They didn't become hockey stars overnight." His mom said, "You can learn a lot by watching what the **JETS** do." She'd been a **JETS'** fan forever.

Logan and Liam agreed—it was awesome to have a home team.
"The greatest team in the league," said Logan.

The **JETS** are great skaters …

They make big plays …

They shoot. They score …

… and make a million saves.

Liam wondered how he could ever play as good as the **JETS**.

"Let's get to The Forks. Game on!" said Logan.
Easy for him to say, thought Liam. *Logan hardly ever misses the net.*

Like always, it was a great day for hockey. Liam was a good skater.
He could play forward. He could play defence. He got lots of shots on goal.
But, like always, Liam just couldn't score.

"A hockey team needs goals to win, but goals aren't everything."
Liam wasn't sure what the man at the rink meant. "If you ask a Winnipeg **JET**,"
the man went on, "he will tell you winning is important, but also that you ...

… have fun

… believe

… play like a team

… always try your best

… never give up

… and be proud when you play well."

Liam told Sophia, "I'm glad we have a goal-scorer like you on our team."
"Thanks," she said, "but you help set up all the plays." And Liam understood that
being the best player isn't what matters—it's being part of the team that counts.

Then something wonderful happened. "We're going to a **JETS'** game!" Logan yelled.
It was the best surprise they'd ever had.

And there was one more surprise, too.

"Isn't that the man from The Forks?!" asked Ethan.

It had been the greatest day.

All the next week, Liam practised and practised.

His dad said, "All **JETS'** fans know persistence pays off."

And it did for Liam, too!

ABOUT THE AUTHOR
Holly Preston

Holly is a journalist, radio host and award-winning documentary producer. She creates children's picture books for professional sports teams. Holly hopes Jets' fans will enjoy having a book that celebrates their home team and encourages young fans to find a love of reading.

ABOUT THE ILLUSTRATOR
Val Lawton

Val Lawton is an artist and children's book illustrator, and The Home Team is her 18th book. This is the third time she and author Holly Preston have teamed up to celebrate Canadian sports.

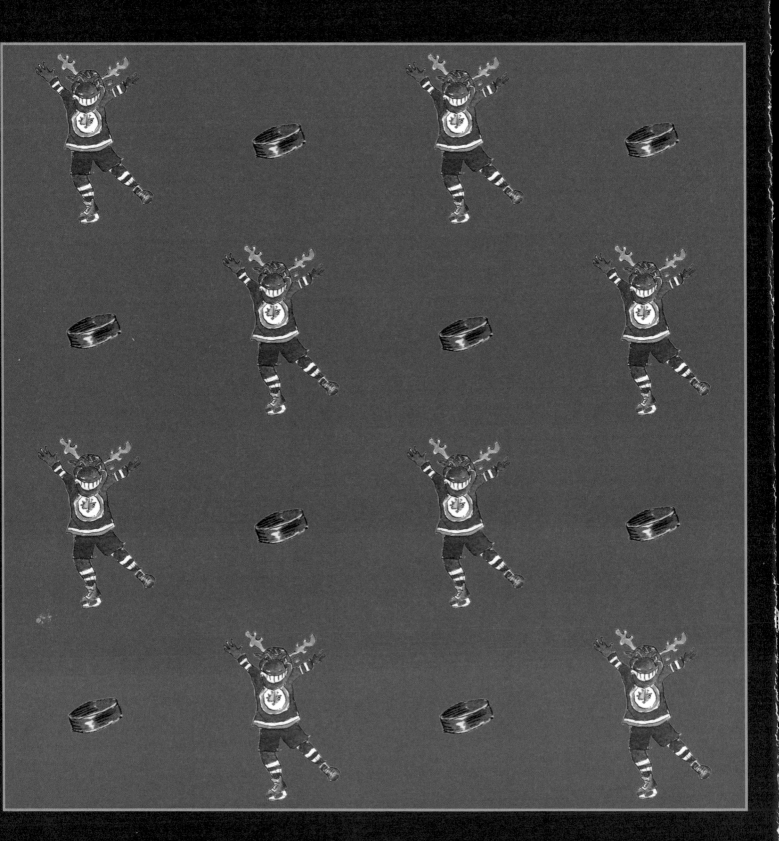